Beautiful Brown

Dona Herweck Rice

Publishing Credits

Rachelle Cracchiolo, M.S.Ed., *Publisher*
Conni Medina, M.A.Ed., *Managing Editor*
Nika Fabienke, Ed.D., *Content Director*
Véronique Bos, *Creative Director*
Shaun N. Bernadou, *Art Director*
Carol Huey-Gatewood, M.A.Ed., *Editor*
Valerie Morales, *Associate Editor*
Courtney Roberson, *Senior Graphic Designer*

Image Credits: All images from iStock and/or Shutterstock.

Teacher Created Materials
5301 Oceanus Drive
Huntington Beach, CA 92649-1030
www.tcmpub.com

ISBN 978-1-4938-9814-5

Printed in Malaysia
Thumbprints.24704

brown

as a

penny

 as a 

brown path

 as a 

brown moth

 as a 

brown bird

brown as a  pinecone

 as a 

brown mountain

 as a 

brown squirrel

 as a 

brown bear

 as a 

brown walnut

 as a 

brown cookie

High-Frequency Words

a

as